6x 8/24 7/20

D0443627

Queen for a Day

Queen for a Day

Retold by Brandi Dougherty

Random House 🏠 New York

rhcbooks.com

ISBN 978-0-7364-3825-4
Printed in the United States of America
10 9 8 7 6 5 4 3 2 1

Queen for a Day

prologue

For some time, Rapunzel had been itching to escape the confines of the castle, and her lady-in-waiting, Cassandra, knew just what to do. Cassandra's father was captain of the guard, and she had an adventurous spirit that Rapunzel, her best friend and charge, shared.

As the princess of Corona, Rapunzel had so many royal duties that every once in a while she needed a break. She wanted a glimpse of the outside world—she wanted to feel the wind in her hair and the freedom that came along with doing something on her own. She'd spent the last eighteen years locked inside a tower, and she didn't like feeling trapped inside the castle!

So one day, Cassandra helped Rapunzel sneak beyond the kingdom's walls without her royal guards. She took her to the site where the miracle Golden Flower had grown—the one that had healed Rapunzel's mother and enchanted Rapunzel's hair. A stone marker had been placed there to commemorate the flower and its importance, but now dark clusters of strange, crystalline rocks had cracked right through the marker and popped up all around the area. The rocks reached toward the sky with sharp, dangerous-looking points.

Cassandra's hazel eyes glistened as she told Rapunzel about the mysterious appearance of the rocks the year before. No one knew what they were or why they had appeared. Besides that, Cassandra went on, the rocks were indestructible.

To prove her point, she struck one with her sword, her short, wavy black hair rushing around her face with the force of the impact. But the

sword shattered instead of the rock! Rapunzel couldn't believe it.

When Rapunzel approached the rocks, they began to glow! She reached out to touch one, but the blue light became so intense that the crystal exploded, knocking the girls backward and creating a blond streak in Rapunzel's short brown hair. At that moment, the rocks began to sprout in aggressive bunches, sending Rapunzel and Cassandra running for safety.

As Rapunzel ran, her hair changed color from the dark brown she'd become accustomed to, to the sunlit blond she'd known all her life. Rapunzel hadn't had blond hair since Eugene had cut it to save her from Mother Gothel. But in an instant, Rapunzel's golden locks unfurled behind her, quickly reaching the full seventy-foot length they had been for most of her life. Her hair had returned!

Rapunzel and Cassandra scrambled to safety across the crumbling bridge that led back to the kingdom. As soon as they'd put some distance between themselves and the rocks, they breathed a sigh of relief. The crystals had stopped growing, but the sharp edges pointed menacingly in their direction—like a warning.

chapter

1

It was a beautiful morning in the mountains of Corona. Birds were chirping. The sun was shining. A bunny rustled through the brush, sniffing at the crisp air. She twitched her nose and peeked out from behind a tree, then made her way to a cluster of low-hanging berries for a morning snack.

Suddenly, crows flew across the sky, cawing loudly. The bunny's ears went back as she looked up with concern. The crows scattered ahead of a dark mass of storm clouds. Wind and snow gusted in enormous waves across the serene landscape. It was a blizzard!

Quirin was working the field in Old Corona on the outer edge of the kingdom. Hearing the birds' loud caws, he turned his tall, hulking frame and peered up in time to see the clouds moving steadily across the horizon toward his village.

The giggle of a young girl distracted him. She was climbing a tree and reaching for a flower at the end of a branch. Suddenly, a strong gust of wind blew through the valley, knocking her off balance. The girl cried out as she fell toward the ground, but Quirin caught her just in time. He set her down and the girl glanced up at him, once again happy and safe. Then she ran off, past an outcrop of mysterious black rocks. The formation was made of dark crystalline shards jutting out of the earth in strange bunches. Another villager stood staring at the rocks as Quirin approached the village square.

"What do we do, Quirin?" the man asked, gesturing to the ominous cluster in front of him. "My home! These rocks are destroying everything in their path!"

They were the same rocks Rapunzel and Cassandra had encountered on their adventure beyond the kingdom. Now the rocks were encroaching on Quirin's village.

More citizens of Old Corona gathered around, looking expectantly at Quirin. He was a leader in the village, and the others sought answers and reassurance from him. Quirin held up his hands. "Take ease, friends." His deep voice boomed across the square, strong and sure. "Our situation may seem dire, but we mustn't lose hope."

"But what are they? Where are they coming from?" a man asked.

Another, lighter voice spoke up from the crowd. Villagers parted to reveal Varian, Quirin's teenage son. "I've been studying them, and I think I've discovered a vulnerability in their alchemical makeup," he said, his black hair flopping into his eyes. A pair of safety goggles was perched on top of his head, making his big ears stick out. He wore thick black gloves and an apron. Varian was an inventor and loved to use science to solve problems. The spreading of the rocks was his biggest challenge yet.

Quirin moved close to his son, eyeing the villagers around them. He bent down and lowered his voice, hoping the others wouldn't hear him. Varian looked small and a little awkward next to his father. "Son, I told you. Leave those rocks alone!" he murmured, his square jaw jutting toward Varian.

"Yeah, I know, I know, but something has to be done, and I think I might be on to a solution." Varian's face brightened, excited at the prospect of a new discovery. He wanted nothing more than to make life easier for his dad and his fellow villagers through his inventions. He'd even tried to bring hot running water to Old Corona by using steam-powered tankers in the caverns underground. But his project hadn't gone exactly as planned.

"Something *is* being done," Quirin responded, straightening up again. "In fact, I plan to travel to see the king this afternoon about this very matter."

Varian beamed. "Oh! Well, um, then . . . can I . . . can I come with you?" He blinked his blue eyes hopefully at his father.

Quirin let out a gruff sigh, but then he saw the excited look on his son's face. "Very well," he said. "You can travel with me."

Varian could hardly believe his ears. "Really? Yes. YES!" he cried, pumping his fists. "Road trip! We're going to see the king!" Varian sang, and danced in place. "I'll pack ham sandwiches!" he added before dashing off to get ready for their journey.

"Hmm," Quirin mused. "Yes. But in the meantime, stay away from those rocks." His voice was stern and concerned.

Varian had stopped a few feet away. "Okay, but, um . . . that's getting harder to do by the minute," he said as he looked around and realized that even more rock groupings had sprung up all across the square. They were dotted between homes and trees, covering the village. Just as he was about to take another step, the point of a new black rock sprang up inches from his face. They needed to fix this problem—and fast!

At that very moment, the king, queen, and Rapunzel sat in the throne room listening to their royal subjects. The king was in the middle, with the queen and Rapunzel on either side. While Rapunzel and her mother looked petite in their grand, royal chairs, the king took up most of his ornate seat. A line of people extended across the room and out the door. Rapunzel was still getting used to being a princess and everything it entailed. She wanted to learn as much as she could from watching her parents handle all sorts of situations.

Next up to speak to the king was Feldspar the cobbler, who stood on the carpet several steps below them. "Your Majesty," he began. "Ever since you repaved the roads, wear and tear on people's shoes is at an all-time low."

On Rapunzel's shoulder, Pascal yawned, his long pink tongue stretching out. The chameleon was bored. Rapunzel gave her friend a sympathetic smile. She had made herself as comfortable as possible in her throne. Her blond braid cascaded to the floor. She wore a fancy dress fit for a princess, with puffed, striped shoulders, and pink sleeves, and a corset underneath, but her bare feet peeked out from below the hem of the silken fabric. She hated wearing shoes and still hadn't gotten used to cramming her feet into those awkward contraptions after having gone barefoot in the tower for so long.

In the eighteen years Rapunzel had spent with Mother Gothel, the woman had never allowed her to leave her home. She was locked high above the ground in a soaring stone tower. So now, Rapunzel loved any opportunity to experience new things—especially with her feet. She liked the way they felt on the ground exploring different textures of stone, grass, dirt, or water. As a princess, she was expected to learn all the royal customs and traditions, but wearing shoes was one thing she wasn't ready to do.

"Not one person has come into the shop all week," Feldspar continued.

Rapunzel looked to her father for his reaction.

"I see." The king smiled, his dark mustache lifting slightly. "Well, we can't very well *unpave* the roads, can we, Feldspar?"

The cobbler looked down, disappointed.

"However . . . ," the king continued, glancing quickly at his wife, who smiled. The queen's green eyes sparkled, mirroring Rapunzel's. "It occurs to me that the royal guard is in need of new boots. Do you think you might be of service, sir?"

"Might I?" Feldspar's face lit up. "Why, of course, Your Majesty!"

Feldspar hurried away, delighted. Rapunzel tapped her father on the shoulder and leaned over to whisper, "Do the guards *really* need new boots?"

"Uh, no," the king admitted. "But the livelihood

14

of our local businesses is worth the extra cost."

Pascal nodded in agreement. Rapunzel smiled. "Wow!" she said, in awe. "I've learned so much from shadowing you these last few days."

"Good. Because you must be prepared for any contingency while we're gone," the king said, pointing a finger at her with a serious expression on his face.

"Uh, Frederic," the queen interjected. "We're going to be away for hardly any time. We deserve a little break. I think she can manage." The king and queen were headed to their mountain retreat for their anniversary. Rapunzel would be in charge while they were gone.

"Oh, I know she can," the king agreed. "After witnessing the supreme judgment she exercised while defending Attila, there's not a doubt in my mind."

Rapunzel thought back to the opening of the pub thug Attila's bakery. The pub thugs were a group of ruffians Rapunzel had met when Eugene took her to the Snuggly Duckling tavern. She'd been afraid of them at first, but they all became fast friends—especially when the pub thugs helped Eugene escape the castle to rescue Rapunzel from Mother Gothel.

Attila had always dreamed of being a baker. He made the most delicious cakes and pastries, but the villagers were afraid of him and the big, scary helmet he wore over his face. No one had wanted to give the former criminal a chance—except Rapunzel. When Uncle Monty's Sweet Shoppe was vandalized, the evidence seemed to point to Attila as the culprit. Only Rapunzel believed in him and was able to prove his innocence.

Rapunzel beamed at the memory of helping her friend. "But," the king said, interrupting her reverie, "that doesn't mean a father can't worry."

Queen for a day, thought Rapunzel, smiling to herself. She could handle that.

chapter

2

Eugene stood in his room looking in the mirror. He dipped his finger in a pot of ink and drew a crown on the mirror, right above his head. Positioning himself directly beneath the crown, he studied his reflection, looking satisfied.

"What are you doing?" asked Lance, walking into the room and startling Eugene out of his daydream. Lance was a former thief and an old friend of Eugene's who now lived and worked in the castle.

Eugene turned to face him. "Since Rapunzel is *pretty much* the queen for a couple of days, that makes me *pretty much* the king." Eugene was much smaller and shorter than his husky friend, but Lance's big stature and hearty laugh only added to his charm. Eugene often argued that he was more handsome than Lance, but that was up for debate.

"Pray tell, Thy Majesty, what has thou planned to do with thy newly bestowed might?" Lance asked with an exaggerated bow. His gold earring glinted in the light.

"Ha! Well, I thought you'd never ask." Eugene grinned, then glanced down at the ink now covering his hands. "I figured I'd start small," he continued, rubbing his hands together to try to get rid of the ink. "Take a dip in the royal pool, try on that weird cape-y thing, take a little snooze on the throne, and then from there"—Eugene's brown eyes widened—"I can move on to bigger stuff. You know . . ." He paused and stroked his goatee. "Make a few decrees, negotiate an accord, proclamate a . . ." Eugene scratched his head, ruffling his floppy dark brown hair. "A proclamating thing."

"You're outta your head," Lance replied.

"You're outta your head, *Your Majesty*," Eugene corrected him, crossing his arms with a satisfied smirk.

"Right . . . ," said Lance. "I'd like to see you flex some of that new monarchy muscle." He paused and then broke into laughter, bursting Eugene's bubble just a little bit.

Eugene glanced back at himself in the mirror and at the crown drawn there with a slight frown on his face this time.

Later that day, Quirin and Varian stood in the hallway outside the throne room. They were waiting to speak to the king.

"Okay, Dad," Varian began, moving around with anxious energy. "What's our strategy? I mean, I tried to get a sample of the rocks to show the king, but they just won't cut." Varian had discovered the same thing Cassandra and Rapunzel had—the rocks were indestructible.

Just then, Quirin was motioned forward into

the throne room. Turning toward his son, he said, "Wait here while I speak to the king."

"Dad, I think I should go with you to help explain the scientific–"

"Varian," Quirin interrupted, pinching the bridge of his nose with frustration, "children have no place in court."

"But I . . ." Varian looked down, stunned by his father's words. "I'm not a child . . . ," he said, his voice barely above a whisper.

Quirin patted Varian's shoulder as he walked into the room, leaving his son speechless and alone.

He approached the king. Rapunzel stood to the right of the throne, while the advisor to the king, Nigel, was on the left. The queen was occupied with other royal duties.

"Quirin, my old friend." The king smiled. Rapunzel smiled, too. She loved hearing the delight in her father's voice. "What brings you from Old Corona Village?"

"Your Majesty," Quirin started. "Old Corona is facing quite the dilemma."

"Oh?" Now the king looked worried.

"Yes," Quirin continued. "It would appear that this year's harvest has proven quite bountiful!"

As his father spoke, Varian peeked in through the side door of the throne room to listen.

"So much so," Quirin chuckled, "that I humbly request more land to accommodate such bounty."

Varian's eyes grew wide. His father was *lying* to the king!

Nigel quickly consulted the scroll he held behind his back before leaning close to whisper in the king's ear. "Your Majesty, we've received no such reports from Old Corona."

Rapunzel and Pascal listened intently, concern on their faces. Rapunzel looked from her father to Quirin, who held his polite bow in front of the king.

"Hmm . . . ," the king murmured before falling silent for a while. Finally, he went on. "Quirin,

I'm pleased to hear how well Old Corona is faring. I'm even more pleased to grant your request." The king stood up from his throne. The large golden sun medallion around his neck—the symbol of Corona—glinted in the light.

Quirin raised his head and smiled. "Thank you, Your Majesty," he said before exiting the room.

Nigel and Rapunzel stared after him, surprised. From her shoulder, Pascal gave Rapunzel a confused shrug. In turn, Rapunzel glanced at Nigel and he shrugged, too.

Varian met his father in the hallway. "Dad, none of that was true!" he said as he chased after him. He stepped in front of Quirin. "Old Corona is being destroyed!"

"Old Corona will endure," said Quirin. "You'll have to trust that I can handle this." And with that, he continued down the hall.

But Varian wasn't satisfied. He grabbed Quirin's arm to stop him again. "How? How can I *trust* when my own father just lied to the king's face?"

Quirin bent to Varian's level and gritted his teeth. "That's enough, Varian!" he hissed.

Varian was shocked. His father's tone was serious in a way that he didn't hear often. "Yes, sir," he said quietly.

This time Quirin kept walking, leaving Varian in the hallway, confused and saddened by his father's actions.

Just then, Rapunzel came out of the throne room and was pleasantly surprised to find her friend standing before her. But she soon noticed that something wasn't right. "Varian? Is everything okay?" She touched his arm lightly.

Varian pulled away. "No. No, it's not!" He turned to her and went on. "Rapunzel, we came to see your dad about the rocks in Old Corona."

"Yeah, but your dad just said . . . ," Rapunzel started, gesturing back toward the throne room.

"My dad lied." Varian looked at the floor. "Things have gotten worse."

"How much worse?" Rapunzel asked, a little out of breath.

Varian hung his head even lower. He pictured all the destruction his village had endured because of the rocks. Homes had been ruined and crops destroyed, and wells were unusable. The rocks sprang up everywhere with no regard for what lay in their path. One crystal had even speared a young girl's teddy bear. "A lot worse," he whispered.

"Don't worry," Rapunzel said, looking him in the eye. "I haven't forgotten about our agreement."

Rapunzel had first met Varian after she and Cassandra had visited the original site of the mysterious rocks. Once they were safe and sound back in the castle, they started to seek out answers about the return of Rapunzel's hair. The first thing they learned was that Rapunzel's hair was now unbreakable.

Cassandra decided to take Rapunzel to meet Varian, who they'd heard was a magical wizard. At first, they were intimidated by Varian's lab, but it turned out that he was just a science-obsessed teenager. He *wasn't* a magician, but he proved to be smart and inventive, and he'd created a staggering number of chemical compounds and machines that could do amazing things.

So, in an effort to find answers, Varian had strapped Rapunzel into one of his crazy inventions and run a lengthy series of tests to figure out what her hair was made of. They learned that Rapunzel's hair no longer had the healing powers it once had. But just as they were about to receive the full results of the tests, Varian's lab began to crumble. They barely managed to escape the explosion unharmed. The only thing that saved them was Rapunzel's hair, which had created an indestructible bubble around them.

Later, Varian revealed that he had also seen the strange rocks. Once Rapunzel and Cassandra heard this, they returned to Varian's village to see the rocks for themselves. Sure enough, the black shards were the same as the ones they'd encountered outside the kingdom's walls. And when Rapunzel got near the cluster of rocks, both the rocks *and* her hair glowed!

Rapunzel revealed to Varian that her father

had forbidden her to speak to anyone about the rocks. And Varian confided that his father knew something about them, too, but he wouldn't talk about it. Right then and there the friends vowed to discover what was happening with the rocks and why.

Now, standing in front of Varian, Rapunzel understood his concern. "We're going to figure out the mystery behind these rocks. Together," she said, as sure of her vow as ever. "Just give me until my father returns." She grabbed Varian's shoulders and met his gaze. "Everything's going to be okay. I promise," she added, smiling.

Varian smiled, too, his face full of hope for the first time in days.

chapter

3

Early the next morning, Rapunzel stood at the front gates of the castle, ready to see her parents off on their anniversary getaway.

"We hope to make it to the mountain retreat by noon," the queen told her.

Rapunzel wrapped her mother in a big hug. "I'm so excited for you guys!" From his perch on Rapunzel's shoulder, Pascal joined in on the hug, squealing excitedly.

"Take good care of them, Max," Rapunzel called to Maximus, a horse in the royal guard and Rapunzel's friend. Max neighed from the front of the carriage. Pascal winked and gave him a thumbs-up.

Eugene stepped up next to Rapunzel. "You two kids have fun, now!" he said with a laugh. Lance and a line of pub thugs stood behind him and Rapunzel. Each of them wore a wide grin. There was Attila, with his metal helmet; Hook Foot, with a scary-looking hook for a foot; Big Nose, the hopeless romantic; and Vladimir, the biggest and most menacing thug of all, who liked to collect ceramic unicorns.

The king eyed the oddball cast of characters warily and furrowed his brow with concern. "Are you sure you'll be okay, Rapunzel? Your mom and I can always stay. We have plenty of anniversaries to come, you know."

"Frederic!" the queen said, exasperated.

Lance stepped forward and put his massive arms around Rapunzel's and Eugene's shoulders. "Don't worry, Your Majesty. We've got everything under control."

Pascal looked from Lance to the king and shook his head. He wasn't convinced that Lance or the pub thugs had *anything* under control.

"Uh, th-thank you," the king stammered, not quite sure who Lance was. "That's comforting." Just then, something caught his attention and he glanced down at Lance's feet. "I'm sorry, but are those *my* shoes?"

Lance laughed sheepishly and then backed away to hide the fancy shoes he'd found in the king's closet.

Rapunzel moved toward her father and put a hand on his shoulder. "I won't let you down, Dad."

The king touched Rapunzel's cheek and looked deep into his daughter's eyes. "I know you won't, sweetie. Now, remember, you'll discover when you become queen that many voices demand to be heard, but when all is said and done, the voice in your heart is the one you should follow."

Rapunzel nodded and smiled.

The king and queen stepped into the carriage. Rapunzel, Eugene, and the others waved goodbye until it disappeared beyond the castle gates.

As soon as the coast was clear, Lance yelled, "Kitchen raid!" and raised his fist in the air.

"Woo-hoo! Kitchen raid!" the thugs shouted as they threw up their hands and ran with him toward the castle.

Cassandra drew her sword with a frustrated grunt and began to chase after them. She wasn't about to let the castle fall to pieces while the king and queen were away. Even though her official title was lady-in-waiting, Cassandra's dream was to join the castle guard. One day, under her father's direction, she would help protect the citizens of Corona.

Seeing her intent, Eugene quickly tried to step in. "Hey, hey, hey, Cassandra!" he called, running after her. Sometimes she was a little *too* enthusiastic about the idea of being a guard.

Rapunzel and Pascal remained with their eyes fixed on the gates. Rapunzel sighed softly, letting her father's wise words sink in. She was ready to take on the responsibility of keeping things at the castle running smoothly.

Later that morning, Rapunzel stood in the throne room. "So," she started, her face full of excitement. Pascal rubbed his hands together from his perch on her shoulder, ready to get going. "Whatta we got, Nigel?"

Nigel unrolled a long scroll. "Well, first there's the royal council to hear out your subjects' concerns." As he spoke, the scroll unfurled to its full length, rolling all the way down the stairs and across the room. Rapunzel's eyes widened in surprise and Pascal's mouth hung open. This was A LOT more than she'd expected.

Rapunzel rallied. "Well, all right. The people of Corona have a problem? Consider it solved!" Pascal nudged her and pointed to the door. A steady stream of Coronians pushed through the entryway and into the throne room.

Rapunzel's face fell as the crowd continued to expand. "Wow! A little longer than yesterday, right? But nothing I can't handle!" Rapunzel's smile returned and she put her hands on her hips.

"Actually, Princess," said Nigel, "word got out

that *you* would be receiving subjects, and, well, we had quite a turnout." He chuckled.

In fact, the line of subjects wound all the way around the castle! Men and women filled every hallway and curved around every corner. They talked excitedly about their chance to speak with the princess.

Meanwhile, in Old Corona, Varian watched through the window of his lab as Quirin gathered with the villagers in the square.

"I've made the good king aware of our problem, and we have his blessing," Quirin told the concerned crowd. He had lied to the king about the reason for needing more land. It wasn't to grow more crops. Instead, the land would be used to relocate homes away from the encroaching rocks. What the villagers didn't know wouldn't hurt them. They all cheered and surrounded Quirin, thanking him.

Varian slammed his fist down and walked

away from the window. He stood next to a towering crop of rocks inside his lab. He touched one of the spikes and sighed.

Varian's raccoon, Ruddiger, worked his way between Varian's legs and nudged his feet, making quiet chattering sounds. Varian picked him up.

"Running away isn't going to fix the problem," Varian told him. "These rocks must be stopped!" Varian set the raccoon on one of the rocks. Ruddiger struggled to hold on to the slippery surface and began to slide down the length of one of the crystals. "Okay, Ruddiger, so what do we know about them?" Varian continued as he paced the room. Ruddiger slid farther down the shard, looking increasingly alarmed. "They're unbreakable, they're somehow connected to the princess, and"—he dove into a pile of scrolls and pulled one out—"worse yet, they're growing at an exponential rate."

Varian unrolled the scroll and pressed it flat across the table to reveal a map of the kingdom on which he'd plotted the movement of the rocks. "Within a matter of months they will have reached the castle," he said, pointing. Ruddiger made another chattering noise from where he was now wedged between two crystals.

Varian plucked him from the rocks and the raccoon settled onto his shoulders. "Now, physical force has no effect on the rocks," he went on. "But they've yet to reckon with the awesome power of alchemy!" With a dramatic gesture, Varian threw back a tarp from one of his tables to reveal lab equipment on which a mysterious liquid was brewing. The liquid was heated in a beaker over a flame until it bubbled up through several chambers, coils, and orbs and then poured into another beaker. Varian drew a dropperful of liquid from the second beaker and took it over to the rocks. He put on his safety goggles and let a bead of the liquid fall onto one of the crystals. The liquid immediately burst into flames.

"Whoa, whoa!" Varian cried, looking around for something to quell the flames. Ruddiger jumped from his shoulders and hid.

"Son, are you okay in there?" Quirin asked from outside the door.

"Yes, Dad. I just . . . uh . . . dropped a book!" Varian shouted, covering the crystal with a tarp to try to stamp out the fire. A small explosion welled up under the tarp and let out a loud *POW!* "It's one of my . . . BIG books!" he added, clutching the tarp, eyes wide.

Back at the castle, Eugene was overseeing the pub thugs as they made renovations to the gazebo in the royal garden. Vladimir and his friend Shorty carried in a ladder, while Attila began painting. Ulf, the resident mime, leant his support by making imaginary paint strokes in the air.

"Good! Now, don't forget the trim on the left," said Eugene, looking up from the plans in his hand and pointing.

Lance approached him. "Really taking advantage of that king clout, aren't we, Your Majesty?"

Eugene turned toward his friend. "Blondie

asked me to do a check on the renovations as part of her queenly duties." Lance looked skeptical.

"It's an important job," Eugene added defensively, glancing back at the plans. Suddenly, a bucket of paint landed upside down on his head. "Ow!" he cried, looking up with a grimace.

"Sorry, dude. My bad!" Hook Foot called down from the top of the gazebo.

Lance looked amused. "It's good to be king, huh?" he said as he patted Eugene on the shoulder, pretending to console him.

"Okay," Eugene said, jabbing Lance in the chest. "You wanna see me flex a little muscle? Watch this. All right, boys," he called to the workers, clapping his hands to get their attention. "Let's get the lead out. After we wrap this up, I'm gonna need some renovations to my room."

Vladimir held the bottom of a ladder as Shorty climbed up. They both stopped to listen to Eugene and exchanged a dubious look.

Eugene continued. "I'm thinking sunroof." Within seconds, another bucket of paint sailed down and landed on his head. "Doh!" he cried.

"Just for the record, that one was on purpose," Hook Foot called again.

"Mmmm-hmmm," Lance added.

Inside the castle, Rapunzel stood looking down at the line of people waiting to see her. Cassandra put her hand on Rapunzel's shoulder. "Are you sure you can handle it?" she asked.

Rapunzel drew in a deep breath to steady herself. "Yeah, of course," she said, full of enthusiasm. There were so many decisions to make. Rapunzel loved feeling independent for the first time.

"I've got this," she said to herself as she took her seat on the throne, ready to meet the royal subjects.

"Princess Rapunzel," Nigel called. "May I present your most humble subjects." He bowed and gestured toward the throng of angry, shouting people gathered before Rapunzel.

First there was a land dispute between sheep

farmers. One farmer didn't want the other farmer's sheep grazing next to his. Then there was an argument between a barber and a fiddle player. The barber complained that he was having trouble concentrating on cutting hair because the fiddle player never stopped playing! Next there was a problem with the village being overrun with kittens eating everything in sight. It was up to Rapunzel to solve these problems for everyone.

"Right," Rapunzel said, standing up from the throne. She told the sheep farmers that the land was public and that they needed to share it. To help drown out the noise of the fiddle, she gave the barber a pair of royal earplugs. And she decreed that they would feed all the kittens right there in the castle square. "Fair?" she asked.

"Yes!" the people cheered.

Rapunzel handled each issue with confidence, and the people were pleased.

"She's got a knack for reigning," Cassandra said to herself as she carted away the box of kittens the villagers had brought to prove their claim. She was impressed by how steady and sure Rapunzel seemed. But as she walked down the line, which continued out the door, she became a little worried. There were so many problems to solve! Nevertheless, she had faith in her friend. "She's got this. No prob."

Rapunzel met with subject after subject until, finally, the room cleared. "Is that the last one?" she asked Nigel warily.

Nigel opened the door and peeked out. "Well, not *exactly*, Your Highness." And with that, another angry mob rushed forward. The sheep farmers were back. They had tried sharing the land, but now they couldn't keep their sheep separated and didn't know whose animals were whose!

"Oops," Rapunzel said.

The barber was also back. He couldn't hear his customers' requests through the earplugs Rapunzel had given him to mask the fiddle playing. He pulled a paper bag off a man's head, revealing a pink Mohawk!

Other villagers reported that the kittens were

quiet and happy with full bellies, but now rats were running all over the kingdom! Rapunzel cringed.

"No more interviews!" Nigel cried, pushing the people out of the throne room.

Finally, Rapunzel was alone. She slunk down on the throne and shook her head. "Gosh, what a disaster," she said to Pascal. "And everybody knew it." She stood up. "I had one job to master and I completely failed." She stepped into the hall and looked up at a painting of her and her parents. "I was so certain I could handle this." She touched the picture, a regal image of her as the princess of the royal family of Corona. "But I'm not ready. Not yet."

chapter

4

That evening, Rapunzel sat on her balcony, looking out over the kingdom. She was thoughtful and quiet as she brushed her long golden hair.

"So, how was your first day on the job?" Eugene stepped outside, his boots clicking across the floor. Without a word, Rapunzel ran into his arms for a hug. "Whoa," he said. "Is everything okay?"

Rapunzel sighed. "I'm just . . ." She gazed at the sky and sighed again. "How am I ever going to do this?" She turned and stared out over the edge of the balcony.

"Hey, hey," Eugene said gently. "Relax. You only have to hang in there one more day. Your parents will be back soon."

Rapunzel groaned. "I know." She turned toward Eugene again, flinging her hands out in frustration. In the process, she knocked her hairbrush to the ground. She felt as if she couldn't do anything right! "But it's not tomorrow I'm worried about. Someday this is going to be my job *every day*. And I'm . . . I'm not sure I can handle it."

Not only that, Rapunzel still wasn't sure she *wanted* to handle it. Taking care of the kingdom was a lot of responsibility. There was a part of her that just wanted to have adventures and go wherever the wind might take her. Meanwhile, Eugene had had nothing but thrills and adventure his whole life, and now he was ready to settle down. In the castle. With Rapunzel.

Eugene paused and then picked up Rapunzel's hairbrush. "Blondie, come on. Look at all the amazing things you've done since leaving the tower. Do you think you would have been able to do any of them if you'd stopped to worry about *how* you were going to do them?" He handed her the hairbrush and she smiled. "I know you didn't choose this," he continued, touching her shoulders. "But you of all people should know that if life hands you lemons . . ."

Rapunzel stared at him, not understanding why he'd trailed off. "Yes? Finish that thought," she prompted.

Eugene realized that Rapunzel had probably never heard the expression "When life hands you lemons, you make lemonade" before. Her life had been so sheltered in the tower for all those years. He quickly ditched the saying and went on. "My point is that you, more than anyone I've ever known, are able to make the best of any situation." Eugene took her hands in his. "You're the queen. Go with it!"

Rapunzel's face brightened just as something soft and cold landed on her nose.

"Uh . . . snow?" Eugene asked.

Rapunzel stood staring up at the sky. A look of wonder danced across her face. "Oh my gosh!" she whispered. "I've never actually been outside when it was snowing!" She spread her arms wide as she opened her mouth to let snowflakes land on her tongue.

Eugene shivered. "Well, I have, and, you know, I'm not a fan. I mean, it's cold, it's a pain, it ruins your day." He looked at Rapunzel, who spun in a circle with her arms out. "It's like Cassandra, but warmer," he added. Eugene never missed an opportunity to slip in a jab at his frenemy.

Rapunzel stopped, her eyes flashing with an idea as she ran inside.

"Hey! Where are you going?" Eugene asked.

"To enjoy life's lemons!" Rapunzel called back.

"That's my girl." Eugene smiled. Then a gust of cold, wintry wind slapped him on the back. He shivered violently this time, then hurried inside. "I hate snow," he growled before shutting the doors.

In no time, the snow was falling fast and heavy. It was just as snowy on the narrow path where Max was pulling the king and queen in the royal carriage. He had a look of focused concentration on his face while he trudged up the mountain toward the retreat. But as the snow thickened, Max was unaware that the ground beneath his feet was beginning to crumble from the weight of the carriage.

The queen looked out the carriage window at the blustery weather. A tall hat and scarf covered her long brown hair. She smiled. "Oh, it's beautiful!" she gasped with almost as much wonder in her voice as Rapunzel had. "I can't recall the last time it snowed this much." She turned toward the king and took his hand. He joined her in admiring the wintry scene.

"Looks like there's more to come," he said. His voice, unlike the queen's, was laced with concern.

"I don't know, Arianna, maybe we should return to the castle."

"Frederic, I know you're worried about Rapunzel . . ."

As the queen spoke, several enormous icicles fell from an overhang above the path. They landed right in front of Max, who startled and pulled back, letting out a frightened neigh. The carriage swerved behind him. Max planted his hooves as best he could, but he was beginning to lose his footing on the slippery ground.

The queen continued, ". . . but she's going to be—" Suddenly, the carriage slid toward the edge of the mountain! Max struggled to dig his hooves into the path, but he couldn't regain his traction on the icy snow. He tried racing forward instead, but the reins holding the carriage weren't strong enough to bear the straining weight. In an instant, one of the reins snapped and half of the carriage slid over the edge, sending the queen falling through the now-open door. She cried out, glancing behind her at the snowy abyss below.

The king grabbed her hand just in time. "Arianna!" he shouted.

The queen tried to steady her breath as the king hauled her up into the carriage. They clung to each other with terror on their faces. Max turned his body toward the carriage and pulled with all his strength, desperate to keep the carriage on the path. But the second strap gave way with an awful *SNAP,* and the carriage tipped over the side of the cliff and fell down the mountainside. Max ran to the edge and watched in horror as it disappeared from view.

Meanwhile, at his house in Old Corona, Quirin pulled a heavy trunk from a hidden nook in the wall. He glanced around, brushing the dust from the trunk's lid to reveal a strange symbol. It was the same symbol that was tattooed on his hand:

a circle with three lines extending from the center and down to the left, almost like a comet. He nervously looked over his shoulder again to make sure no one was coming. Then he kneeled and opened the trunk and pulled out a knight's helmet that also had the same symbol etched into the metal. He caught his reflection in the shiny surface and grimaced.

As he stood up, still holding the helmet, he glanced out the window at the menacing rocks. The sharp points of the crystals were aiming straight toward the castle far in the distance. Worry shadowed his features.

But Quirin's face softened as something near the window caught his eye. Moving toward it, he smiled. Hanging on the wall was a picture of him and a beautiful woman looking down at Varian as a baby, their faces full of joy. He fixed his eyes on Varian's sweet, innocent face and sighed.

At the same time, Varian continued his research in his lab.

"Never give up, Ruddiger," he told his raccoon as he banged his fist on the table for emphasis. "Our last formula didn't deliver quite the reaction we'd hoped." He mixed two solutions together and held up the flask. "So what? The important thing is we got a reaction!" Varian moved over to the grouping of rocks and was about to pour a drop of the compound onto one of the shards.

Just then, Quirin opened the door. "Son," he said, startling him. Ruddiger ran to hide beneath the table. "I just want—"

"Oh, oh!" Varian cried, flustered by his father's sudden appearance. He didn't want Quirin to know that he'd continued to experiment with the rocks. As he turned to face his dad at the door, he accidentally flung some of the compound in the flask onto the rocks behind him without realizing it.

Quirin quickly entered the room and approached his son, a look of anger on his face. He didn't see the spilled compound, either, but there was no way he could miss the rocks. "Varian, I told you to stay away from those rocks!"

Varian held up his hand. "I know what you said, but—"

"Then there should be no misunderstanding!" Quirin yelled as he led Varian away from the formation. Neither of them noticed that the formula began to sizzle and bubble against the crystals. "Now listen to me when I—"

"No!" Varian shouted back, shoving his father away. "You listen to me, Dad!"

Quirin was shocked by his son's intensity.

"Our village is dying," said Varian. "You think running away from the problem is going to fix it? No. These rocks aren't going away!"

Quirin pinched the bridge of his nose. He was tired and frustrated, not to mention conflicted. "I know, Varian. But there's more to them than you can possibly imagine!"

"Then why won't you tell me?" Varian asked as the bubbling on the rocks increased behind him.

Black rocks have appeared throughout Old Corona. Varian and his dad, Quirin, decide to travel to the castle to tell the king.

Rapunzel prepares to take over royal duties from her parents while they go on vacation. She is going to be queen for a day!

Rapunzel promises to help Varian get rid of the mysterious rocks.

Rapunzel worries that she won't be able to help the people of Corona.

Back in Old Corona, Varian tries to use alchemy to destroy the black rocks.

Quirin gets trapped! Varian travels to the castle—he needs Rapunzel.

Rapunzel declares a snow day in Corona! Everyone has fun in the winter weather.

But a fun snow day quickly turns dangerous. It isn't safe to stay outside.

Maximus returns to the castle alone. The king and queen are missing!

Eugene, Lance, Maximus, and the Pub Thugs offer to find Rapunzel's parents.

Varian asks for Rapunzel's help, but the kingdom needs her now. Rapunzel has to break her promise to Varian.

Eugene and the gang spot Rapunzel's parents at the bottom of a cliff. This rescue mission turns treacherous!

The blizzard gets worse by the minute. Rapunzel calls for an emergency evacuation.

Rapunzel convinces Cassandra to help her find the Demaritus device, a machine that could stop the snowstorm.

Rapunzel and Cassandra find the Demaritus device, but a rock gets stuck in the gears!

Pascal risks his life to save Corona.

The machine works! The blizzard stops. Everyone returns to the castle, safe and sound.

Being queen for a day was tough, but Eugene reminds Rapunzel that she will always have her friends by her side.

Quirin walked away. "Dad! I deserve to know!"

With his back to Varian, Quirin removed his glove and looked at the symbol on his hand. "I'm sorry, son. You're not ready." He turned to look at Varian and noticed yellow shards growing from the rocks at an alarming rate. They were about to engulf Varian!

"Varian, watch out!" Quirin shouted. He ran forward and shoved Varian away from the rocks. Varian collapsed on the floor and then looked up in horror to see that his father's arm was glued to the gooey rocks. Quirin struggled to break free.

Varian ran to his father's side. "Hold on, Dad! I'll get you out!"

Quirin pushed him away again. "No! Stay back!"

They watched as the molten rocks oozed and grew and then crystallized, encasing even more of Quirin's arm. Varian ran toward the door. "I'm going to get help!"

"No, son, don't!" Quirin called, but Varian was

already out the door, running through the snow toward the castle. Quirin slumped against the weight of the lava-like substance as it trapped him where he stood.

chapter

5

Rapunzel stood on the balcony above the castle courtyard, ready to address the people of the kingdom, grinning from ear to ear. She had on a long, bright pink winter coat trimmed with light pink fur, and matching pink boots and earmuffs. Cassandra was on one side of her, a satisfied smile on her face. Eugene was on the other, looking a little more unsure. Both were bundled in winter gear.

Rapunzel stood up extra tall and shouted to the crowd. "Loyal subjects of Corona, as your temporary queen, I officially declare today . . . a snow day!" She threw her arms in the air and everyone cheered loudly.

61

Rapunzel and Cassandra hurried off, excited to enjoy the winter wonderland. Eugene stepped up to add to Rapunzel's decree. "And as your temporary king, I . . . ," he started. But all he heard was laughter. Looking down, he realized that everyone was already hard at work—having fun! Families made snowmen together. Shorty glided across the ice like a professional figure skater. And—*WHAM!*—a snowball hit Eugene right in the face. He looked over to see the group of girls who liked to braid Rapunzel's hair giggling and waving.

Eugene waved back and forced a smile. "Nice shot, kid," he mumbled as he walked past Lance. Lance chuckled.

Eugene clutched the banister and tried to make his way down the slippery stairs. They were coated with ice, basically creating a giant winter slide. "Easy. One step at a time," he told himself. He really hated this weather!

Just then, Rapunzel glided by. "Wheeee!" she cried. She was followed by Lance, who shouted joyfully as he slid down behind her. Eugene let go of the handrail and tried to skate, too. But he slipped and skidded and almost fell, grabbing the handrail again just in time. He wore thick gloves and a fur-lined hat that covered his ears, but he was still cold. The earpieces flapped up and down like a pair of wings as he tried to regain his balance. "Ugh, is there anything worse than snow?" he grumbled.

Cassandra skated up sideways like a pro, her arms crossed. She had on pants and tall boots, and a shawl with a fur-trimmed hood covered her shoulders and framed the smug look on her face. "Hello, your royal travesty," she said.

"I spoke too soon," said Eugene.

"Playing make-believe king isn't panning out like you'd hoped, is it, tiger?" she asked.

"It's working out just fine, thanks," Eugene said, letting go of the railing to face her. Then he promptly fell on his backside and slid the rest of the way down into a giant snow pile at the bottom of the path.

Cassandra pushed off from the banister and skated to a stop in front of Eugene's feet. The rest of him was still buried in the snow. "You know, it's not like this king thing gives you any actual power," she reminded him, bending toward the snowbank that covered him. "But even if it did, it might be nice to stop trying to exploit it and start trying to put it to good use."

Cassandra glided away as Eugene shook the snow from his face. "Yeah, no, that's okay. Don't help me up."

He was still brushing the snow from his clothes when Rapunzel flew by again, chasing a group of laughing kids. She slipped and Eugene caught her just before she fell.

"Whoa!" she cried. "Thanks, Eugene. Guess I'm still getting used to this weather. Does it always snow this much?"

"Only once," a deep voice boomed in response from nearby. "At least, according to legend." A large figure held a torch in front of a metal drum, where a fire burned so that people could warm their hands. It was Xavier the blacksmith.

Rapunzel and Eugene exchanged a curious glance. "Legend?" Rapunzel asked as they moved closer to the fire along with several others.

"The legend of Zhan Tiri," Xavier said as he dipped the torch into the metal drum, bringing the fire to a roar. Rapunzel was mesmerized by the glow as Xavier began to tell the story. "Eons ago, an evil warlock, Zhan Tiri, had a deep hatred for Corona and cast a spell that caused a blizzard to sweep across the land. The storm destroyed everything in its path. All would have been lost had it not been for the ancient engineer and inventor Lord Demaritus. Using both magic and science, Demaritus created a massive subterranean machine deep in the Corona mountains. This mighty device had the ability to change the direction of the wind, and it pushed the flurries out to sea. The kingdom was saved. After that, Zhan Tiri disappeared. Some say he's long gone, but others say his anger and hatred turned him into the storm, and now he's simply waiting to strike again."

"Waiting?" Rapunzel asked. The princess's eyes were wide and the fire glowed in their reflection. "For what?"

"For Corona to be at its weakest," Xavier replied, poking the fire.

"For Corona to be at its weakest," Rapunzel repeated. Eugene was still and quiet by her side. "But it *is* only a legend, right, Xavier?" she asked warily.

Xavier's laugh was deep and gruff. "My dear," he said. "Every legend is born of truth."

The crowd stood still, looking a little stunned. Finally, Vladimir slowly started to clap, unsure how else to respond. He stood at the fire directly behind Shorty, looking like a giant statue. The twisting horns on the sides of his helmet extended from his head like handlebars. The crowd remained silent.

"Bravo!" Eugene piped up. "Way to keep the

party going, Xavier. Tell me, have you ever con-
sidered visiting sick children to help lift their
spirits?" he asked sarcastically.

Just then, a strong gust of wind and snow blew
in, surprising everyone and extinguishing the fire.

"Whoa! Okay . . . I think for everyone's safety,
we should all head indoors," Rapunzel shouted
over the wind.

The crowd agreed and began to head inside.
But the sound of a slowly approaching horse
made everybody turn. Rapunzel squinted against
the blowing snow to see who it was. Max stag-
gered out of the blizzard and into view, letting out
an exhausted grunt.

"Maximus!" Rapunzel cried, running to his
side. "Are you okay? And where . . ." She looked
behind Max to where the carriage should have
been. "Maximus, where are my parents?"

Max stared into Rapunzel's eyes, then lowered
his head toward the carriage's broken reins. The
captain of the guard kneeled beside him, picking

up one of the reins. "Looks like there was an accident up on the mountain," he said.

Rapunzel's eyes widened in fear. "Accident?"

The captain of the guard stood up. "Rapunzel, I think your parents are in grave danger."

chapter
6

The village square was deserted as the wind and snow whipped shop signs back and forth and tore at window shutters with its bitter cold. All the villagers had taken shelter in the castle. In the throne room, Cassandra stoked a roaring fire. Pascal stirred sugar into a cup of tea and handed it to a grateful citizen. Rapunzel made her way through the room to ensure that everyone was warm and comfortable.

She approached Nigel, exhaustion and worry on her face. "Nigel, I need to go look for my parents."

"But, Your Highness, you're the queen! You can't just leave your kingdom at its darkest hour."

Nigel pulled Rapunzel aside and spoke gently. "As much as it pains me to say this, their chances in elements as hard as these are . . . Well, let's pray that your parents found shelter before the worst of the storm hit."

"But we can't just let them freeze!" the princess cried.

"My dear, going out in that weather now is a virtual death sentence. You cannot go!" Nigel responded.

"He's right, Rapunzel." Eugene stepped forward. The pub thugs, Lance, and Max stood behind him. "You can't. But we can."

"But you just heard Nigel. It's a death trap!" Rapunzel exclaimed.

Lance moved closer. "Look at us, Princess. If the rest of the world had its way, each and every one of us would either be on the run or locked up somewhere."

"But your parents had the heart to give us a second chance," Big Nose chimed in. "A chance to prove ourselves and get on the right path."

"The least we can do is give them a second chance of their own," Attila added.

"Listen to them," Eugene said, holding Rapunzel's shoulders. "There's no other option. The mountains made for a great hideout back in the day. I know those roads better than anyone. Face it: we're the men for this job. Besides, even a make-believe king has got to make himself useful." Eugene exchanged a meaningful glance with Cassandra, who had just walked up next to her father, the captain of the guard.

The captain took a step forward. "Your Highness, it really should be the guards who go."

"If this storm keeps up, things could get ugly. And the kingdom will need its guards," Eugene argued.

The captain nodded, knowing that Eugene was right. He turned to Rapunzel. "Your Highness? It's your call."

Rapunzel looked into Eugene's eyes and fought back tears. She grimaced at the horrible choice she had to make. The corners of Eugene's mouth tipped up in a small, comforting smile. Finally, Rapunzel whispered, "Go."

Eugene hugged her tightly. "We'll be back. I promise." He kissed her forehead and moved toward the door, the pub thugs, Lance, and Max following.

Max stopped and turned back to Rapunzel, nudging her lowered head with his nose. Rapunzel nuzzled him close. "Bring them home, Max," she said quietly against his soft fur. She clutched her hands to her chest with worry as he walked away.

Pascal climbed onto Rapunzel's shoulder while Cassandra squeezed her into a hug. "Don't worry, Raps," she told her friend. "If anyone can find your parents, they can."

Back in Varian's lab in Old Corona, Quirin struggled against the molten rock as it continued to spread across the room and encase his entire body. A table tipped toward him. He stretched out and grabbed a piece of parchment and a quill pen before they fell to the ground out of his reach. He scribbled a quick note and held the paper over his head as the ooze continued to overtake him. The note began: *Son . . .*

At the same time, Varian raced through the blizzard to the castle. He wore a hooded patchwork cape and a scarf and held a lantern to guide his way through the blinding snow. All he wanted was for his father to trust him and believe in him. He hoped that making it to the castle and bringing help back to Old Corona would convince his father once and for all that the mistakes he'd made could be put in the past.

Varian traveled over icy water, climbed slippery slopes, trudged through dense forests, and crawled in and out of frozen caverns. He even used an old piece of wood to sled down a mountainside. When he lost his lantern, he fastened vials of his various glowing compounds to the end of a long pole to create light—all to reach the castle and get help for his father.

"Just this once, let me come through for you," Varian said aloud, as if speaking directly to Quirin. "Let me make you proud. Let me show you the best in me. Let me give you a reason to believe that I can be trusted. That I can be an adult."

Cold and exhausted, he crested yet another hill. As the castle finally came into view, Varian had a renewed burst of energy that carried him forward. He was ready to save his father and save the day!

In the throne room, Rapunzel paced restlessly. Cassandra stared out the window at the raging blizzard. With a screech, Cassandra's owl flew up to the window and pushed himself inside, blowing snow to the floor. Rapunzel rushed to close the window against the storm. The owl landed on Cassandra's outstretched arm and screeched again—he had a message.

"Cass, what is it?" Rapunzel asked.

Cassandra closed her eyes and hung her head for a moment before meeting Rapunzel's concerned gaze. "The worst of the storm is yet to come," she said quietly.

The owl flew farther into the room and positioned himself next to Pascal in front of the fire. He shook his tail feathers to warm them. Pascal smiled, warming his tail, too.

Nigel and the captain of the guard approached Rapunzel and Cassandra.

Nigel spoke first. "Unless we do something, Rapunzel, the whole island will be buried. Our only hope is to call a state of emergency, evacuate to the shelters on the mainland, and pray the storm blows over."

Rapunzel pictured the castle perched on the small island, the village of Corona huddled below. Only one narrow bridge connected the kingdom to the mainland. "We'll never be able to get everyone to safety in time." She sighed and began pacing again. "That can't be the only way. . . ." Suddenly, she stopped short and turned to face the others. "What about Xavier?"

"Your Highness," Nigel gasped. "With all due

respect, lives are at stake here. We can't go chasing after *fairy tales* in our darkest hour!"

Before Rapunzel could answer, Nigel's shouts were replaced with even more desperate ones from Varian. He burst into the throne room, two guards at his heels. "Princess Rapunzel!" he cried.

The captain of the guard grabbed him by the arm as the other guards caught up. "Sorry, Princess, he ran right past—" one of the guards started to say, just as Varian struggled out of the captain's grasp.

"Wait, it's okay. It's okay!" Rapunzel held up her hand.

Varian gasped for air. "Rapunzel, my dad's in danger! You're the only one who can help! Please, you have to come to Old Corona with me. Now."

Rapunzel looked past Varian to Nigel, Cassandra, and the guards awaiting her instructions for the citizens in the castle. So many people were depending on her to make a decision. She met Varian's desperate gaze again. Then she took him by the arm and led him from the room. "Varian, what's wrong?"

"The rocks—they're encasing my dad," Varian explained.

"Encasing?" Rapunzel repeated in disbelief. "What are you saying?"

"Come see for yourself. You can help! I know you can. You have a connection to those rocks!" Varian ran toward the door, expecting Rapunzel to follow.

Rapunzel squeezed her eyes shut and looked at the floor. "Varian, we're in a state of emergency here. I'm sorry, I . . . I can't help you. Not right now."

Varian stopped and turned back. "No! No, no, no. Listen to me. It *has to* be now. My dad doesn't have much time. You're the only one who can help. Rapunzel, please!"

Nigel approached. "Your Majesty. Whatever the boy's problem, it must be set aside. The storm's growing stronger by the second."

"No!" Varian cried, grabbing Rapunzel by the shoulders.

"We need you to make a decision," Nigel continued.

"No! Please, Princess!" Varian was on his knees now, pleading frantically.

Nigel stepped back and motioned for the guards to come and help.

"You promised you'd help me! You promised!" Varian shook her. "Rapunzel! Please!"

"That's enough, boy," the captain of the guard said as he and the other guards grabbed Varian and led him away from the princess.

"Please don't hurt him!" Rapunzel called out, cringing at Varian's words. She remembered her promise to him, and she'd never thought she'd be forced to go back on it.

The guards dragged Varian down the hallway kicking and screaming. "Rapunzel!" he tried one last time. "My dad needs help!"

Rapunzel covered her mouth in shock.

"Rapunzel!" Varian continued to cry as he disappeared around a corner. "You promised. You promised!" His words echoed back to her, and she buried her face in her hands. The burden of Varian's cries was too much to bear.

chapter

7

High on the mountain pass, the king and queen huddled together inside the carriage. They put the last wooden piece of a broken carriage wheel on their small fire. Icicles hung from the king's beard, and their breath huffed out like frost as the blizzard continued to rage around them.

The queen looked at her husband, concern knitting her brow. "How's your ankle?"

"My ankle's the least of our worries," the king replied quietly. "The kingdom—there's so much left to do."

The queen put her hand on his shoulder. "Fred, she's going to make a great queen."

The king nodded, pulling her into a fierce hug.

"Happy anniversary, sweetheart," she said.

"Happy anniversary, Arianna," the king replied.

Meanwhile, Max led Eugene and the others up the mountain path to search for the king and queen. The steady wind and blowing snow made it slow going. They could barely see and had to put all their weight against the wind, but the group pushed forward.

Suddenly, Eugene looked ahead of Max and gasped. "No!" he cried, seeing a wall of snow burying the path in front of them. "No!" he shouted again in frustration.

Max hung back from the group and peered over the edge of the cliff, trying to see through the blizzard. His nose worked quickly, smelling the air. Finally, the snow cleared just long enough for him to spot the small glow of the king and queen's fire down below. He neighed loudly.

Eugene and the others ran to his side. Eugene beamed. "There they are! Good job, Max."

Max nodded proudly.

"Great," Lance said. "But how do we get there?"

Eugene looked around, searching for any possible path. "We'll have to reach them by taking that ridge." He pointed down to a narrow, dangerous-looking ledge.

"That tiny little thing?" Lance replied, eyes wide.

Max grunted and led the way.

"That is one determined horse," Lance muttered moments later as he took his first step onto the ledge.

The men walked slowly in single file along the treacherously narrow path. Their backs were pressed against the mountain as they shuffled along. The packed snow splintered and gave way under their feet, but they kept going.

Lance sucked in his belly, but he still couldn't see where he was stepping. "I knew I should have stopped at four donuts this morning. Curse you, crullers, and your alluring delectability!" he shouted into the wind.

"Shhhhh!" Eugene warned. "You want to bring that down on us?" He pointed to the precarious bank of snow high on the cliff above their heads. Loud noises could easily lead to an avalanche, and that was the last thing they needed.

Back at the castle, Rapunzel was in the war room, where her father had always gathered with his guards during emergencies. She huddled around a miniature model of the kingdom with Cassandra, Nigel, the captain, and several of the guards. They were trying to formulate a plan to keep everyone safe. All of a sudden, a blast of wind howled from outside, followed by a loud crashing sound. The entire room vibrated as one of the castle turrets was ripped away by the storm! Things were getting worse by the minute.

A young guard burst into the room, doubled over from running as fast as he could. "Your Highness!" he gasped. "I've just come back from the docks. Between the wind, the snow, and the surging tide, no ship is leaving Corona."

Another strong gust of wind blew open a nearby window, filling the room with blustery snow. Rapunzel raced over to close it. She stayed there, facing away from the others in the room.

"Princess, I'm sorry," Nigel said sternly. "If we're going to act, it must be now!"

Rapunzel kept her hands on the cold glass and looked out at the kingdom. There was so much uncertainty. She wanted to do the right thing and make sure everyone was safe. The responsibility was staggering. She bowed her head and closed her eyes. "Evacuate the island."

"You heard the princess!" the captain ordered. The guards fled the room and rushed out to the square. In no time, they began to help panicked subjects gather food and kegs of heating oil. It was chaos as wagons were loaded with supplies and families layered on hats and gloves, hurrying to make their escape.

Rapunzel and Cassandra stood shivering at the castle doors as they watched the villagers prepare to leave the island.

"I hope I'm making the right decision," Rapunzel said, worry spreading across her face.

Cassandra sighed and put her hand on Rapunzel's shoulder. "You're not, Rapunzel. . . . You're making the *only* decision."

They walked through the square, where Rapunzel stopped to help a young boy who had slipped on the ice. She smiled at the boy's mother, then turned to Cassandra. "This evacuation . . . it doesn't feel right, Cass," she said.

"Raps, this is exactly what your dad would do if he were here," Cassandra told her.

Rapunzel let out a long breath. "If he were here, he would tell me to follow my heart." Suddenly, she looked over Cassandra's shoulder and smiled.

"What?" Cassandra followed her gaze to a fire glowing in the blacksmith's shop. "The Demaritus device?"

Rapunzel nodded. She felt hopeful and positive.

"Just so I'm clear," Cassandra continued, holding up her hands. "We're talking about the mythical subterranean machine that can magically control weather?"

"Are you in or out?" Rapunzel replied, her voice steady. They had to try. And she believed finding this device was the right answer.

Cassandra looked over her shoulder again. "Looks like we've got a blacksmith to visit."

Inside his shop, Xavier pushed aside objects on his shelf to reach a hidden scroll. "Princess, I never said the Demaritus device was real *for sure*."

"I know, Xavier, but 'every legend is born of truth,' right?" She echoed his words back to him. "What if Zhan Tiri's curse is real, and this storm won't let up until Corona is destroyed? Even an evacuation won't help then. That machine might be our only hope!"

Xavier turned to look at Rapunzel. Her face glowed with determination. Pascal sat on her shoulder, looking equally determined. "Please,"

Rapunzel said. "If the legend is true, where would the Demaritus device be?"

Xavier dipped a torch into the fire. "I have an idea," he said, holding up the flame.

At the edges of Old Corona, Varian raced through the snow. He stumbled, then picked himself up again. Finally he made it to the village and ran toward his lab.

"Dad! Dad! I'm back!" he shouted as he burst through the door. "Dad, the princess refused to help, but I–" He stopped. His father was fully encased in the molten rock. "Dad?" Varian dropped his makeshift torch and raced forward, slamming his fists into the rock. "No, no, NO! Dad! Dad!"

Varian's eyes filled with tears as he stared at his father, frozen in time, his arm raised, still clutching the note he had written.

chapter

8

Back on the treacherous mountain pass, the rescue party continued their dangerous search for the king and queen.

"There!" Vladimir shouted, pointing to a lower ridge. The carriage and a dim fire were barely visible below them.

Eugene stared down at the fifty-foot drop and the icy wall that separated him from the king and queen. "Vlad, get me the rope," he said.

The group secured two ropes, and Eugene and Lance each tied one around their waists. The pub thugs held the ropes steady as the two men stepped over the edge and began to rappel down the wall. They were making good progress until Eugene's foot slipped on the ice, sending him falling several feet before the others could regain their hold on the rope. He gasped and struggled. He was scared, but he fought hard to find his footing again. When he did, he let out a relieved sigh and gave a terrified Lance a thumbs-up.

Up at the top, Big Nose started to sniffle, his nostrils twitching. "Uh-oh. You know what happens when I get stressed . . ." He started to sneeze. "Aaah, aaah—"

Hook Foot put his finger under his friend's big nose. "What are you trying to do, bring the whole mountain down on top of us?" And with that, Hook Foot himself sneezed. "ACHOOOO!" he cried. The sound echoed across the mountains and all around them. Eugene and Lance stopped their descent and held their breath. A wall of snow rumbled from the cliff above and began to fall straight toward them.

"Oh man, I hate snow," Eugene mumbled as the drifts crashed down onto their heads.

Eugene and Lance fell to the ridge and were buried in snow. Suddenly, two hands reached out to brush the icy powder off Eugene's face. He spat more snow from his mouth and blinked at the figure above him. The queen smiled down. "Oh! Hello, Your Majesty. We've come to rescue you!" Eugene said, managing a smile.

The queen helped pull Eugene from the drift as Lance called out from another drift next to him. His words were muffled and he struggled to get up, his boots just visible above the snow pile. He was upside down and wrestled to break free. It wasn't exactly how they'd planned to reach the king and queen, but they'd made it. And so far, everyone was okay.

Rapunzel, Pascal, and Cassandra followed Xavier through a dark underground tunnel filled with cobwebs. They rounded a corner, where Xavier stopped in front of a wall. "Huh?" he said, holding up the torch for more light. "According to the legends, there should be a passageway here."

Cassandra put her hand on her hip and sighed. "I knew this would be a waste of time."

Xavier continued forward, studying the rock wall in front of him. He held up the torch again, illuminating a symbol on the stone. It was a large circle with three smaller circles surrounding it— two on the right and one on the left. He pushed the symbol with his hand.

"Come on," Cassandra said to Rapunzel. "If we hurry we can still catch up with the rest of the evacuation and—"

Her words were interrupted by the sound of the stone wall sliding back, revealing a passageway. Xavier grinned as Rapunzel and Cassandra looked on, surprised. "This way," he said, gesturing for them to follow him.

Aboveground, the captain of the guard led the citizens across the bridge to get them off the island to safety. "Keep pushing, people!" he cried as they struggled against the impossible winds. "We can make it!"

The first throng of evacuees had reached the center of the bridge. Just then, a huge gust of wind blew, knocking a horse off balance. The horse was pulling a wagon full of heating oil. The frightened animal bucked against the wind and came loose from the wagon, sending it crashing backward into the side of the bridge. A keg of heating oil bounced away and split open on the ground, making contact with a fallen lantern. In seconds, a line of fire was racing toward the other fallen barrels of oil.

"Everyone get down!" the captain shouted just as the fire made contact with the barrels. A huge explosion erupted around them. The captain lay on the ground, blown backward by the force of the blast.

When the smoke cleared, he could see that an entire section of the bridge was missing. Shelter from the storm lay on the mainland, which was now unreachable. "We're trapped," he whispered.

chapter
9

Rapunzel, Pascal, Cassandra, and Xavier continued their underground trek. Soon they reached what seemed to be a huge, dark cavern. Rapunzel took several steps forward. All of a sudden, the ground began to crumble beneath her feet. She was standing at the edge of an enormous precipice!

"Rapunzel!" Cassandra ran forward and grabbed her friend's arm. "Gotcha," she said, pulling Rapunzel and a frightened Pascal back from the edge. Pascal peered into the blackness and swallowed hard, clinging to the princess.

Xavier stepped up next to them, lighting the

room with the torch. "I think this is it," he said slowly. He walked over to the wall and dipped the torch into a narrow trough. A fire quickly ignited and spread the length of the trough, encircling the cavern with a warm glow. The light illuminated a giant cylindrical apparatus that towered high above them. Levers and round bulbs protruded from all sides.

Cassandra gasped. "I don't believe it."

"Your Highness, the Demaritus device," Xavier said.

Rapunzel led the way down a steep, narrow staircase to the base of the gigantic machine.

"So this is the device that's going to blow the storm out to sea?" Cassandra asked, a little skeptically.

"Not if we just stand here looking at it," Rapunzel replied. "Let's try to get this thing up and running." She used all her weight to push one of the levers that stuck out from the base of the machine. If she could get the bar to move, it would get the machine going. Cassandra and Xavier joined in pushing other levers on the wheel. The bars began to rotate more quickly. The device picked up speed, spinning faster, too. Before long, bolts of lightning began to fly between the bulbs, crackling in the air.

Rapunzel looked up, shading her eyes against the glowing energy that was gathering like a storm of its own. "I think it's going to work!"

The disk spun faster and faster, creating a funnel cloud that reached through the opening in the mountain above them. At the same time, the earth began to tremble from the force of the spinning. The walls started to crumble, sending rocks and debris tumbling downward. A piece of wood fell and knocked along the edges of the device before lodging in one of the giant cogs. The machine ground to a halt. The funnel cloud that had been created disappeared as quickly as it had come.

"You have got to be kidding me!" Cassandra said with a groan.

At the same time, high on the mountain pass, the queen took one last step up the mountainside and reached for Lance's hand. She'd made it to the higher ledge above the wreckage of their royal carriage.

Below, Eugene secured the injured king in a series of ropes attached to a carriage wheel that would carry him in a makeshift swing. "Okay, Your Majesty. This should hold you," he told him.

The queen stood behind Lance, her face lined with worry. Lance nodded at Max and the pub thugs as they began to pull the king up the icy wall. "All right, up there. Steady now," Eugene called.

Halfway through the ascent, the wind started to blow harder, sending the king swaying back and forth. He clung desperately to the fragile ropes that held him.

"Oh no," said Eugene, looking up from the ridge below.

The ropes took another violent turn in the

104

wind, and one of them snapped. The king fell from the harness and began to slide down the side of the mountain. Eugene watched in horror.

"Frederic!" the queen shouted.

The king continued his fall, sliding past where Eugene stood on the ridge. He was about to slip to a depth far below. "Your Majesty!" Eugene cried out, racing across the snow to grab the king's hand just in time. "Hold on!" Eugene pulled with all his might, trying to find a hold for his other hand in the shifting snow. The king dangled over the steep drop as the wind howled and the snow swirled around him. It was impossible to see how far down the drop was.

Up above, Lance watched Eugene struggle to keep his grip on the king. He turned to the other men. "Quick! Help me get down there."

The king could feel his hand slipping from Eugene's grasp. "Eugene, please. Help take care of Rapunzel," he said.

But Eugene wasn't ready to give up. "We're

going to get you out of here," he said between grunts. "Besides, you should know by now that Rapunzel doesn't need anyone to take care of her."

The king's hand almost slipped from Eugene's grip once more. Just then, Lance appeared at his side. "Almost got you . . . ," Eugene said through gritted teeth. With Lance's help, the king was finally pulled to safety.

Back in the great cavern, the gang was determined to dislodge the wood from the cog to get the machine up and running again. They had a plan. Rapunzel unbraided her hair and let it out to its full length. Pascal tied the end of it around his waist like a harness and gave her a thumbs-up. Rapunzel let her hair down slowly, lowering Pascal next to the device so that he could reach the piece of wood. Little did they know that on a mountainside far away, a similar operation was in motion to get the king and queen home safely.

"Come on, Pascal!" Rapunzel encouraged him. She lay at the edge of the precipice looking down at her friend. Her hair had been lowered as far as it would go. Pascal struggled and reached, even sticking out his tongue to get closer, but he just wasn't close enough. He looked up at Rapunzel and shook his head. It wasn't going to work.

"Okay, Pascal," Rapunzel said. "Let me pull you up and we'll figure out some other way."

Pascal looked down at the cog and then up at Rapunzel again. Tears filled his eyes, but along with them was a look of fierce determination.

"Pascal?" Rapunzel asked, getting worried. What was he thinking? Just then, Pascal reached up and untied her hair from around his waist. "No, Pascal!" she shouted.

But the little chameleon let go of Rapunzel's hair and fell to the depths below.

"No! Pascal!" Rapunzel cried again.

Pascal lunged for the piece of wood and

grabbed it as he fell. It came loose from the cog and the entire machine began to spin and generate electricity once more. Rapunzel continued to stare down at where her friend had disappeared. Finally, she stood up. Cassandra steadied her. "Pascal?" Cassandra asked. Rapunzel buried her face in her hands and cried. Cassandra pulled her into a hug.

The whirlwind of blue light generated by the Demaritus device began to grow and push up through the crevasse at the top of the mountain once more. But this time, the energy continued and spread out wider and wider, until it covered the entire kingdom and sucked the raging blizzard into its field of energy. Almost as suddenly as the storm had begun, the wind died down, the snow stopped, and the air began to clear. Frightened citizens who'd been stuck on the bridge clutching their loved ones close as they tried to ride out the storm finally loosened their grasps and took a moment to breathe. They looked up, realizing that the weather was changing. The storm was clearing.

The king, Eugene, and Lance also watched from their place on the ridge. They exchanged a smile, and the king squeezed Eugene's arm in thanks. Then he looked at Lance and did a double take. "Excuse me, is that *my* hat?"

Lance glanced up at the hat on his head with a sheepish look on his face.

Back in the Demaritus chamber, Rapunzel continued to cry. "He's gone," she said, clutching her hair.

"I'm so sorry, Rapunzel," Cassandra said gently as she drew her into another hug.

Xavier stood nearby with his head in his hands as Rapunzel wept. But something at the edge of the precipice caught his attention. "Wait!" he whispered. A small green hand reached up. Then a bruised, battered, and exhausted Pascal slowly climbed into view, gasping for breath. "Look!" Xavier cried.

"Pascal!" Rapunzel ran to her friend. Pascal smiled and let out a little squeak of happiness. Rapunzel swept him up into her hands. She touched her nose to his, happy and relieved to see that her lifelong friend was okay.

chapter
10

When the sun finally appeared again, it glinted off the gleaming white snow. The bunny who'd been tossed around as the storm approached poked her nose out from a snowbank and shook the crystalline powder from her head. In the castle square, shopkeepers dusted the snow from their signs and helped each other shovel their walkways, waving and smiling to their friends. It was a bright new day.

In the castle courtyard, Rapunzel waited, holding her breath. Nigel, Cassandra, and the captain of the guard stood by her side. Finally, the group Rapunzel was waiting for came into view.

Eugene appeared first, followed by Lance and the pub thugs, and finally, the king and queen on Maximus's back. Rapunzel rushed forward into the arms of Eugene. Then her mother and father stepped down and embraced her with just as much love. Rapunzel smiled over her father's shoulder and held out her hand to Max. No one spoke. They were all relieved to be safe and together again as a family.

Later that day, Rapunzel sat in her room, staring out at the snow-covered kingdom. Her journal lay in her lap, open to a page where she'd painted the wintry scene before her now. She looked sad and tired. A knock at the door pulled her attention away from the window.

Eugene appeared holding a pink-frosted cupcake on a tray. "Hey! Celebratory cupcake?"

Rapunzel shut her journal and looked out the window once more. "No, thank you." She sighed.

"Hello?" Eugene was confused. "Blondie, come on! You kicked butt and saved the day. What are you upset about?" He placed the cupcake on the table.

Rapunzel turned to face him. "Eugene, I turned my back on a friend in desperate need," she said, thinking back to the memory of Varian's cries. She shook her head and continued. "I sent the man I love to face possible death. And then I did the same to my oldest friend. I entrusted the entire welfare of Corona to a fairy tale. In a lot of ways, today was the most difficult day of my life."

Eugene frowned. "Sweetheart, what are you saying?"

Rapunzel hesitated. "I . . . I'm not sure I want to be queen."

Eugene looked surprised. Rapunzel turned away again. He came to sit next to her at the window. "I know today was overwhelming. And I can't say I wouldn't feel the same way. But you becoming queen is a long time away. Just know that when the time comes, I'll be right here with you no matter what you decide." Eugene took her hands in his.

Rapunzel smiled and leaned in to hug him. "Thank you for bringing my parents home."

He smiled back. "You got it."

In Old Corona, the new day wasn't as bright. Varian knelt at the feet of his father, still fully encased in the mysterious chemical compound on the rock.

"Don't worry, Dad," he said. "I *will* get to the bottom of this, I promise. I'll make you proud. I'll get the answers and set you free, whatever it takes. And I swear right now that no matter what becomes of me, anybody who stands or has stood in my path will pay." Varian bowed his head and clenched his fists tight. Ruddiger emerged from under the table and watched him, frightened. Varian's eyes were dark and his face was obscured by shadows. "They will pay," he repeated.

Coming Soon

Keep reading
for a sneak peek!

chapter

1

Rapunzel giggled as her father struggled to free himself from a tangle of long yellow streamers. "It's not funny!" King Frederic protested. "Have you any idea how difficult—"

Rapunzel lifted her equally long blond braid before he could finish. She was very familiar with being tangled. Just combing her hair out every morning—before braiding it—took almost an hour!

The king laughed and shared a smile with Rapunzel as she freed him from the streamers. She had been surprised when her father offered to help her decorate the castle courtyard for her nineteenth birthday celebration in a few days. He was usually so serious. It was nice to joke around with him and have fun for once.

Rapunzel and the king finished hanging the streamers and brought out the kites that would line the courtyard. The kites resembled the flying lanterns King Frederic and Queen Arianna had launched every year on Rapunzel's birthday, after she'd been kidnapped as a baby by an evil woman named Mother Gothel.

Growing up, Rapunzel had seen the lanterns from the window of the tower where Mother Gothel had imprisoned her. She would watch the glowing lanterns float through the night sky, wondering what they meant—unaware that they were for her.

Most of the kites were colored gold, but Rapunzel spotted an unusual one, with purple stripes. As she picked it up, a breeze lifted it from her hands.

A moment later, Rapunzel was no longer in the courtyard of Corona. Instead, she was in Old Corona, a village a few miles from where her friend Varian lived. The sun was gone, and clouds

blanketed the sky. Spiky black rocks stuck up from the ground throughout the village.

More rocks burst up around her. Rapunzel stared in shock as her hair began to glow.

"Rapunzel!" a high-pitched voice called. It sounded like Varian.

Rapunzel looked around, searching for her friend. She saw her father standing a few yards away . . . yet somehow still in sunny Corona. She moved toward him—but a wall of rocks shot up, separating them.

A hand grabbed her arm, and she spun around to find Varian beside her. "Help me!" he cried. "You promised!"

But before she could respond, more rocks rose from the earth and surrounded him. There was an explosion of light, and Rapunzel's glowing hair whirled around her. . . .

Rapunzel snapped open her eyes, freeing herself from her nightmare to find she was no longer in bed. She was hanging in midair, suspended above her balcony. Strands of her glowing hair fanned out around her like the legs of a spider and clung to the stones of the castle's wall. The glow faded and the strands broke loose from the stones.

Rapunzel fell. . . .

"Rapunzel!" cried Eugene, Rapunzel's boyfriend, as he rushed into the room. He reached the balcony and caught her just in time. "What happened?"

Rapunzel gazed up at him, dazed and frightened. "I . . . I don't know." Eugene set her down and she hugged him tightly, trying to force away her fear.

She had dreamed about the black rocks before. Each time, they seemed to be coming after her—just as they had in real life when she'd first seen them, on a cliff outside the kingdom.

The rocks alone were menacing, but now it  seemed that even the dreams themselves were dangerous. . . .

In her art studio later that morning, Rapunzel painted the images she remembered from her dream, trying to make sense of them. Pascal, her pet chameleon, sat on her shoulder, watching her fill her latest canvas with thick slashes of black, each one rising to a sharp point.

Eugene and Cassandra, Rapunzel's lady-in-waiting, studied the finished paintings. One portrayed the lanterns soaring off into the sky; another showed Rapunzel's blond hair flying around her head.

Rapunzel knew her dreams were trying to tell her something. "The rocks, my hair, Varian . . . it's as if they're all connected," she explained to her friends. "I have to find out *how*."

Rapunzel first met Varian when she'd asked for his help to figure out why her long hair had returned. Varian was an alchemist, with a laboratory full of potions he'd invented and machines he'd built to test the properties of all sorts of things. Yet he hadn't been able to solve the mystery of her hair.

"What if the dream was a warning?" Eugene asked. "Telling you to stay here, where you're safe?"

She knew Eugene might be right. But if the rocks *were* dangerous, it wasn't only Rapunzel who was in danger.

Shortly after her first visit to Varian, a cluster of black rocks had sprouted up behind his house. Varian had come to the castle not long ago to tell her that more rocks had appeared. She had promised to help him, but a terrible blizzard had hit the kingdom, and she'd been too busy dealing with the storm to keep her promise.

But what if the rocks had destroyed Varian's house in the meantime? What if they had spread through his whole village, as they had in her dream?

Rapunzel remembered another key part of her dream—her father. She needed answers, and if anyone could tell her what was really going on in the kingdom, *he* could.

chapter

2

In the past, whenever Rapunzel had asked her father about the rocks, he had refused to talk about them. But she couldn't let him brush off her questions any longer. It was clear she was connected to the rocks in some way—maybe even responsible for them. She needed to know the truth.

Rapunzel found King Frederic in the throne room, talking to one of his advisors. The king's expression was grim—the opposite of the sunny, smiling face he'd had in her dream.

Rapunzel hurried up to him. "Dad, the black rocks . . . I'm worried they've—"

The king raised his hand. "I thought I made it clear we were not going to discuss this."

"I'm worried Varian is in danger," insisted Rapunzel. "Has anyone been to Old Corona lately?"

King Frederic realized his daughter wouldn't give up until he gave her an answer. He led her over to a miniature model of the kingdom. Dozens of tiny black flags had been pinned in different locations—most of them in Old Corona.

"I've been aware of the rocks for some time," the king confessed. "They posed a real problem: destroying homes, damaging roads. . . ." He plucked out the flags one by one. "Fortunately, we've taken care of them. The rocks have been removed, and the people of Old Corona are all fine."

Rapunzel sighed in relief. Old Corona was safe. "Thanks for being honest with me," she told her father.

The king guided Rapunzel to the door. "Now run along," he said with a smile, looking happy again. "You've got more pressing issues—like planning your birthday party!"

Rapunzel hugged her father and hurried off to report the good news to Cassandra and Eugene.

She found her friends in the courtyard, which had been decorated for her birthday, just as in her dream. A gentle wind fluttered the yellow streamers, and a kite with purple stripes sailed into the courtyard and landed in front of her statue. It was the kite from her dream!

The kite, weighed down by an iron key dangling from its string, floated toward her. Attached to the key was a note. Rapunzel read it.

Rapunzel,

I need your help, now more than ever. I may have discovered the key to the rocks.

Find the bronze cylinder in my lab. But be careful. They're watching, and they'll do anything to stop you.

—Varian

"Who's 'they'?" asked Cassandra.

Rapunzel didn't know. What she *did* know was that Varian still needed her help. King Frederic might have taken care of the rocks, but there was obviously more to the story than he'd revealed. She needed to find out the *whole* truth.

Rapunzel turned to her friends. "We have to go to Old Corona."